BABY ZOO ANIMALS

An Animal Information Book

by Elizabeth Elias Kaufman

FOURTH PRINTING—AUGUST 1988

PRICE STERN SLOAN
Los Angeles

Baby lions are called cubs. This cub is less than a month old. Right now, it is not much larger than a house cat. When it is about a year old, the cub's coat will lose its black color and become sandy.

A baby deer is called a fawn.
Usually, a female deer has two fawns.

Fawns like to eat grass, leaves and some kinds of plants.

As it grows older, a fawn's white spots begin to fade.

A baby hippopotamus can swim soon after it is born. It spends most of its time in the water.

A hippopotamus mother does not allow her baby to go far from her side. Sometimes, she puts the baby on her back when she goes for a swim.

A baby chimpanzee stays with its mother until it is about three or four years old. During that time the mother feeds and protects the baby, and teaches it how to behave.

Chimpanzee babies are very smart. They can be taught to do tricks.

Jaguars are members of the cat family. These jaguar cubs look very quiet and peaceful, but they are dangerous wild animals.

Like all members of the cat family, jaguars have sharp teeth and claws.

Penguin babies are called chicks. The parents feed the chicks until the babies' adult feathers grow in.

The chicks can go into the water to catch their own food once they have these waterproof feathers.

Coyotes are members of the dog family. A coyote baby is called a pup.

One of the things that helps protect the pup is the color of its fur. This color is very much like the color of rocks, making it difficult for predators to see the baby.

Giraffe babies usually stay with their parents until they are about one and a half years old. The mother giraffe has only one baby at a time.

Baby and adult giraffes both like to eat leaves. As the babies grow taller, they can reach the leaves far up on a tree.

Leopards can be dangerous animals. They are extremely powerful and can run very fast.

This baby leopard is called a cub. Although it is not yet fully grown, it has already learned to snarl. When it is an adult, it will have large, sharp teeth and claws.

A female fur seal has only one baby at a time. The baby seal is called a pup.

Fur seals spend most of their time in the water. By the time this pup is three or four months old, it will have learned how to swim.

Wild boars are members of the pig family. These baby wild boars are less than a month old.

The babies will have stripes along their backs until they are about five to eight months old. The stripes will then slowly disappear until the boar is completely either black, brown or gray.

Baby zebras have brown and white stripes. The brown stripes turn to black by the time the zebra is several months old.

Some baby zebras stay with their parents for their entire lives. Others may go off to live on their own when they are grown. Still others leave and return to their parents' herd from time to time. Zebras always live in herds.

This zebra is less than two months old. Its mother will not let it wander too far away from her.

Tiger mothers usually have between two and five cubs at a time. Like all newborns, the cubs are quite helpless, but they will mature quickly.

This cub is old enough to leave its mother's side for short periods of time.

A young grizzly bear cub looks almost like a teddy bear. Don't try to cuddle it, though! Its mother is very close by and will attack anyone or anything that comes near her cub.

This little cub is not even a month old.

These elephant babies are between one and two years old. They were about three feet tall when they were born. They will continue to grow until they are about eleven feet tall.

Elephants become fully grown when they are between ten and fifteen years old. Many elephants continue to grow even after they reach the age of fifteen.

Animal Information Books

Titles in this Series

Baby Animals
Baby Zoo Animals
Bears
Big & Little Animals
Birds
Bunnies & Rabbits
Butterflies
Farm Animals
Horses & Ponies
Kittens & Cats
Lions & Tigers
Monkeys & Apes
Penguins
Pets
Puppies & Dogs
Sea Animals
Wild Animals
Zoo Animals

Published by Price Stern Sloan, Inc.
360 North La Cienega Boulevard, Los Angeles, California 90048

ISBN: 0-8431-1521-1

Printed in Korea.